Blueshift

By Grace E. Robinson

Chapter One

———

The last cargo ship left the Ring. First Lieutenant Elín Hallsdóttir pressed the key to close the outer airlock door.

The computer monitor in front of her showed numbers and graphs tracking the course of the ship as it traveled away from the Ring. Across the room, the gray door leading to the airlock was sealed tight, its tiny window showing barely a glimpse of the vastness beyond.

"The final ship is away, sir," Elín said, glancing down again at the monitor. "It should reach the hyper-driver transport in two minutes. The transport is online and ready to depart once the cargo ship is attached."

"Very good. Thank you, Halls." Bards stepped up next to her. "We did a good job. Six months on this Ring Array and we got every last crew member and piece of equipment sent out on schedule."

Elín looked up at him. His dark face was round with a smile. "Yes, sir," she said. She couldn't bring herself to smile. They had done their job; they stayed on schedule. And now the Ring Array was empty, with only the five of them remaining.

Bards tapped his wrist-gear. "We're done, people. The last ship is away. Timms, Kit, Chang, get in here. Time to give our final report before we shut down the uplink."

"On our way," came Timms' voice over the comm.

Elín took one last look at the monitor. The cargo ship was docking with the hyper-driver. The engines were bright, and in a moment it would be gone. One hyper-driver transport remained, parked in orbit around the largest moon, engines cool in standby mode, waiting for their own ship to leave the Ring. Not much longer now. Only eighteen more standard days, and Elín would leave the Ring Array forever.

Timms came into the control room, his hands stuffed in the pockets of his blue-gray jumpsuit. He leaned against the console nearest the doorway. "So it's just us now, huh?"

"That's right," said Bards.

Elín felt Bards looking over her shoulder at the console. The indicator light for the cargo ship and its transport flashed green, then vanished.

"So, can we celebrate by having a day off?" asked Chang.

Elín glanced up to see Chang sauntering into the room with her usual confidence, as if she owned the universe and was satisfied with her place in it. Elín envied her.

"And do what?" said Timms, looking at Chang. "All the R&R sectors were stripped and shut down weeks ago."

"Sorry, no day off," said Bards. "We've got a little over two standard weeks to complete the final phase of the shutdown. Now that the last of the crew has gone, we're shutting down the uplink to Command. Once a day we'll turn it on to report to Command and downlink any news or updates. You ready, Kit?"

Kit had come into the room behind Chang, quiet as always. He dipped his head, his shaggy bangs falling over his dark eyes. "Ready to record on your mark, sir."

Bards nodded at him and Kit tapped his wrist-gear.

"This is Commander Solomon Bardens of the Dyson-Vanderklein Habitable Ring Array, Epsilon Omega System. The final stage of phase one of the shutdown is complete. My crew are present and reporting in."

Bards looked at Elín. She swallowed before speaking.

"First Lieutenant Elín Hallsdóttir, reporting."

The others reported in.

"Second Lieutenant Adam Timmins."

"Second Lieutenant Jessica Chang."

"Junior Lieutenant Mitsuo Kitagawa."

Bards nodded at Kit. "Send that with the time stamp, then shut down the uplink. Now let's all get back to the main control room for this sector. It's time to start cutting the power."

They boarded a transport tube for the seven-minute ride to the main control room for Sector 68. Gripping one of the support poles, Elín stood with the others in the empty tube cabin. The removal crew had taken the seats out of the tubes, so there remained only the structural poles and the inertial compensators to help them keep their footing as they traveled.

Bards disembarked first, Elín close behind him. Five pairs of boots echoed on the metal floors as they walked the corridors from the tube bay to the main control room. Elín looked around as they walked; the cold gray walls spoke of lifetimes of whispers, light and darkness, and all the madness of life in between. All that was fading now, and would soon be gone, shifting away in the red of retreat. Their route took them past no windows.

Once in the main control room for Sector 68, they all took their stations: Timms and Chang for main and secondary power systems, Kit for long-range sensors, while Elín monitored the internal sensors. Bards stood in front of the master view console, his hands draped behind his back.

"Cutting power to non-essential systems for Sector 68," said Timms, hitting keys on his console.

"Exo-pod is loaded and on its way to our cargo ship in Sector One," said Chang.

"Um, sir," said Kit. "Picking up solar flare activity again."

"It's not going to cause a power fluctuation this time, is it?" asked Timms.

"What would it matter?" Chang said, looking at Timms. "We're shutting down this sector anyway."

"Well, I was thinking about Sector 67...it's, well, we're about to move into that sector. Last time there was a flare—"

"It shouldn't cause any issues with the power," Elín interrupted him, glancing over at Kit's computer screen, then back at her own. "It was a low magnitude flare, and right now this sector of the Ring is on the far side of the planet from the sun."

"That's good," said Bards. "Okay, Timms, is everything powered down?"

"Everything except this room, the main transport tube, and life support."

"Shut off the life support," said Bards.

Lights flashed on the consoles around the room as an alarm sounded. Timms did as was ordered. This was it, then; the final plaintive death throes of the Ring, as they turned off the life support sector by sector. Elín didn't need to look at the screens; she knew that for their crew complement of five, comfortable heat would remain for nearly twenty hours, and healthy oxygen to CO_2 ratios for days beyond that. They would be on a transport tube and well into the next sector long before then.

The faintest flutter went through her stomach as the artificial gravity generators powered off along with the rest of the life support. The Ring's rotation kept the gravity at .87 standard Gs, so there would be little adjustment needed as they traveled from dead sectors back to live ones.

"Okay, people, time to power down the control room for this sector," said Bards. Elín felt his hand coming to rest on the back of her chair. "Halls, Kit—you two need anything else here?"

Kit shook his head. Elín pulled her hands away from the console keys. "All finished here, sir," she said.

"Do it, Timms."

Like a groan and a sigh, the computer screens dimmed and the lights faded. A silence fell as the dull reddish emergency lighting came on. Elín put her hands in her lap and stared at the dark screen in front of her. *That's that*, she thought.

"All right, then." Bards's voice sounded too cheerful. "Good job, everyone. Let's get to the transport tube and head to Sector 67."

STANDARD DAY CYCLE 1, 19:59 GST

Epsilon Omega IV. Dyson-Vanderklein Habitable Ring Array. Such clinical names. Elín leaned against the cold metal railing of the observation walk. This corridor, at the top inner edge of the Ring, was fully windows along the walls and the ceiling. Here the sterile designations held no sway; white clouds, so close and so far, fanned and swirled within the clearest blue of the upper atmosphere.

She frowned at her faint reflection and resumed her walk. Those clinical names were fitting now, and made their evacuation seem timely. All was dying. No, not dying—transitioning. Epsilon Omega IV was changing, merely entering the next phase of its planetary life-cycle. Epsilon Omega IV would continue, but what had been home to Elín was nothing more than an empty hull: the Dyson-Vanderklein Habitable Ring Array, decommissioned.

It was a large enough world to have gathered a natural ring system of its own, but it hadn't. And so, seventy-five years ago the Ring Array had been built around the ice giant planet. During those years, millions of miners, automated and manned, had been gathering hydrogen and nitrogen, ammonia and helium, and rare mastotridium from the frozen atmosphere. But now, the world was changing. The planet was warming, the magnetosphere growing. Not long now, in cosmic time, and the warming atmosphere would expand to swallow the Ring. And so they had to leave.

"What are you thinking about, Halls?"

Elín turned to see Bards beside her. The glow from the planet outside the window turned his brown eyes to amber.

"It's so quiet here," she said.

"I know. On an Array built for a million people, it feels completely abandoned with just the skeleton crew for clean-out. But don't worry—just two more standard weeks, and we'll be leaving too."

"And then what?" *Tell me a lie, Solomon. Tell me I have a home to go to.*

"And then..." he shrugged. "Then we go back to Central Command and get our new orders." Bards' voice grew softer. "After that...maybe we could go home."

Home. The clouds outside the window danced, the hydrogen and helium and methane swirling in a knot. "Where is home, Bards?"

He leaned against the railing, his arm close to hers. He was only a few years older than her, but so much stronger, and he had seen so many worlds. "I've never lived in one place more than three years. But for me, home is the Mother World."

"I've never been there."

Elín felt his gaze fall on her, but she kept her eyes on the planet outside.

"You've never been to Earth at all, ever?" he asked.

"I was born on New Valhalla colony."

He nodded. "I remember; you've told me that."

"My father was transferred here when I was seven. He oversaw all the mines for the southern hemisphere. A few years after that he took command of the entire operation." In life, he was Father; but in death, he was only General Hallur Einarsson, ID number 376-44A23, deceased in the line of duty. What would he think of all this? What would he say to this crew as they prepared the Ring he had died for to become nothing more than a numbered entry in the historical records, just like he was?

Bards was silent. Elín wanted to touch him, but instead she asked, "What is Earth like?"

A smile flashed across his dark face. "Just like every vid you watched in school and every report downlinked from the news. Only better. More *real*. Did you have trees on New Valhalla?"

Elín shook her head.

He turned back to the window. "You've got to see trees one day, Halls. And sunlight—you know, shining down on you from open sky overhead, not just through a window."

She didn't remember the sunlight on New Valhalla; it was a dim, constant illumination from a cool red sun. She looked at Bards from the corner of her eye. What would he look like in the warm light of a yellow G-type sun? Would his dusky, dark skin shine coppery under such light? What would her skin look like? She glanced down at her slender hands holding the steel railing; they glowed pale white-silver in the blue light from Epsilon Omega's star. Would her skin be warm and pink under a different sun?

"I'd like to see the Mother World one day," she sighed. "I suppose it's home for all of us."

"You could say that," he answered. "But first, let's eat something. We shut down five sectors today; we're ahead of schedule. I think we've all earned some food and a good long sleep-cycle."

Five sectors shut down, sixty-three more to go as they worked their way around the Ring back to Sector One. For six months the clean-out crew had been removing everything of value, stripping the Ring down to its bones. Now, all that was left for the five of them to do was sweep through sector by sector, removing the last of the small electronics, loading up the exo-pods, and sending them back to their cargo ship. Behind them they left a silent void, turning off life support, saying goodbye.

"Come on, Halls." Bards put a hand on her shoulder. The warm touch drew her back like gravity.

Elín turned away from the glowing window and followed him back to the barracks. The commissaries for each sector had been long ago stripped bare, so the five of them traveled with their rations, along with their tools and other supplies.

Chang and Kit were sitting on bunks in the barracks. The bunk frames were bare, save for the four where their sleeping rolls had been laid out. Elín hadn't unpacked her sleeping roll yet; she sat down on an empty bunk next to Chang's.

Timms was bent over a bunk, rummaging through one of their packs. "Here we are—dinner is served," he said, pulling out food bars and water pouches. "Oh, I see you found her, Bards." He grinned at Elín.

"We thought you were going to skip dinner, Halls," said Chang, catching the food bar as Timms tossed it at her. He tossed another one at Elín as she sat down; it hit the bunk pallet beside her. Two water pouches landed next.

"I'm not very hungry," Elín said, looking at the food bar in its dull gray wrapper. She opened a water pouch instead.

"For this stuff?" said Chang. "Who is?" She tossed her long black hair over her shoulder and bit into her food bar.

"Not too much longer now," said Bards, unwrapping his bar.

"God, I can't wait to get off this spinning tomb," said Timms, sitting down on his bunk and taking a bite of his bar. "It's bad enough we have to keep eating this stuff." He gestured with his bar. "I've gone six months now without a woman."

"Hey, what are we?" said Chang, waving a hand between herself and Elín.

"Yeah, no offense, but it's against regs and all," said Timms with a smirk, rubbing at the thin beard on his chin. "Besides, call me a softy, but I want *my* woman."

"You're a softy, Timms," said Bards. A mild smile. "Come on, tell us again how hot your girl is."

"Hot as the home sun." Timms tapped his wrist-gear, and a holo of a young woman appeared. The holo twirled her hips and blew a kiss. "She sent me another holo at our last downlink...." His hand hovered over his wrist-gear. "But that one's kinda private." He grinned and vanished the holo.

Bards and Chang laughed. Elín smiled, and so did Kit.

Timms grabbed a water pouch and took a long drink. "As soon as I leave this place, I'm taking all the R&R I've got saved up and we're getting married. Yep, she's taking me off the market, ladies, that's how hot she is."

"You're pathetic, Timms," said Chang.

"So what if I am? What about you? Anybody waiting for your sorry ass when we leave this dump?"

Chang looked down her nose at him. "Wouldn't you like to know?"

Elín smiled. "I know."

"You stay out of this, Elín." Chang pointed a finger at her, a smirk on her face.

"Come on, Chang, be a sport," said Bards.

"Whatever. He's stationed on the Arcturus colony. I've put in a request to get assigned there as soon as this mission is done."

"Aww...now who's the softy," crooned Timms.

Chang threw her food bar wrapper at him.

"Kit's got somebody waiting, too, don't you, Kit?" said Bards, looking over at him.

Kit smiled, and ducked his head in his nervous way. "He's an astrophysical engineer at the testing lab on Beta Kappa VI."

"Of course he is," said Timms, laughing. "Geeks gotta love geeks."

"Your turn, Bards," said Chang. "You got anybody waiting for you out there in the cosmos? Or are you wild and free?"

Elín watched as Bards' face softened, and his eyes grew far away like stars. "There's somebody. At least, somebody I'd like to think might be waiting for me."

"But you don't know for sure?" said Timms. "Man, we've been here six standard months. She's probably given up on you."

"Probably." Bards looked at Timms, and then at Chang, and Kit. Elín moved her gaze to find her food ration as his eyes moved her way.

"All right, Halls," said Timms. "You got a lover out there?"

Elín looked at Timms, taking in Bards' face just beyond. She felt only silence inside. "Everyone I ever knew lived here."

Chapter Two

—

Sector 33. Over half of the Ring was dead now. Eight more standard days and they would leave, taking their breath with them. And Elín would never see the Ring again.

She pushed a plastic crate into the exo-pod. The tiny craft was filled almost to capacity with the remaining salvageable materials from the Ring—circuitboards and wires, glass and plastic and metal, all in scraps. The shell of the Ring was all that remained. In two standard months, the big construction ships would come and take that apart as well. Anything that was left after that would be swallowed up by the expanding atmosphere; it would be as if the Ring had never existed.

"Halls, is there room for one more crate?" said Chang, coming up behind her.

Elín turned. "What size? You might be able to squeeze it up there near the top."

With a grunt Chang hefted the crate above her head and shoved it into the pod. "Just barely fits. I guess that means we're done here."

Chang slid the pod's hatch closed. Elín punched in the code into the panel, hit the button to close the airlock, and the exo-pod slid away into space. It would take nearly two standard days for it to reach the ship waiting at Sector One.

Chang tapped her wrist-gear. "Pod's away, Bards. Sector 33's secure. We—"

A vibration shuddered through the floor and the lights dimmed.

"What the hell?" said Chang.

Elín left the docking room and hurried out into the corridor. Timms was coming towards her, a wrench in his hand.

"Was that another damn solar flare?" he said, waving the tool.

Static buzzed from Elín's wrist-gear. She twisted the frequency dial. "Bards? Kit? Do you read me?"

"...major solar...activity..." came Kit's voice in between bursts of static.

Elín twisted the dial again. "Say again, Kit? Bards, do you read me?" She looked up at Timms and Chang, who had joined her in the corridor. "Let's get to the control room."

The lights continued to flicker, and Elín heard the whine of the air circulators as their power flagged. When they reached Sector 33's control room, both Kit and Bards were there.

"What's happening?" Elín asked, sitting down at a console next to Kit.

"Magnetic disturbances are off the scale," he said.

Timms looked over Elín's shoulder as her screen came up. "More flares, huh?"

"No," said Bards, peering down at a third console. "Way too big for that."

"A coronal mass ejection," said Elín, frowning at the readings. The numbers jumped with static across the screen, but she could still read it. "That burst was just the first wave. The bulk of the emission should reach us in about two minutes."

"Where are we in the Ring's rotation right now?" asked Chang. "Don't tell me we're on the sun side."

"This sector is just entering the penumbra of the planet," said Elín. "So we shouldn't get the worst of it."

"The sun isn't supposed to hit its peak for years," said Chang. "I'm pretty sure that's what the briefing doc said."

"The Epsilon Omega star has an eighty-three year cycle," said Elín. "The peak is still four years away, but flares and coronal mass ejections can occur at any time, especially as it nears its climax." The static lines cleared from her screen, so she tapped a key to bring up a current reading. "Doesn't look too bad; we'll probably experience a few hours of power fluctuations, minor system glitches. We should be all right."

"You've lived here a while, Halls," said Timms. "What was it like last time?"

Elín looked up at him. "The last peak was seventy-nine years ago, Timms. This Ring wasn't built...my father wasn't even born yet."

He pursed his lips. "Right. I knew that. Sorry. Wasn't listening."

Chang punched his shoulder. "Idiot."

"Coronal mass impact in five seconds," said Kit.

Another shudder raced through the floor. Elín saw the walls trembling as the lights dimmed. Her console screen went dark. Seconds later the walls groaned and the lights grew bright again.

"I think that was the worst of it," said Kit. His console screen had revived, but all the others stayed dark. "Communications might be disrupted for a while, though; the magnetic interference is still heavy in the area."

"Keep us updated on any changes." Bards patted Kit on the shoulder. "So where are we for finishing up this sector?"

"We're done, sir," Elín said, standing up. "Chang and I sent the exo-pod just before the first power fluctuation."

"Very good." Bards smiled at her. "Well, let's get out of here. Timms, shut off life support for Sector 33."

"Wait, wait. Maybe we should check the transport tubes first," said Chang. "If we have a 'minor system glitch,' it'll be a long, dark walk to the next sector."

Several of the console screens came back on. "It looks like the transport tubes are at full power," said Kit, checking another screen.

"Right," said Bards. "Timms?"

"Yes, sir." Timms typed the command and hit the switch, and the lights went down again.

They walked down the corridors towards the tube, and Elín felt the floor still shuddering beneath her boots. *I'm sorry,* she thought. *You shouldn't have to die like this.* Blue-hot fire, stripping away what was left on the bones of the Ring. But was it better than being pulled apart, panel by panel, circuit by circuit, crated up and recycled?

"Hey, Halls…" Chang murmured as they boarded one of the cabins on the transport tube. "You look worried."

Elín brought her eyes to meet Chang's. "I'm fine; just…tired."

Chang frowned at her. "Look, you and Kit are the scientists of the group." She glanced towards the front of the cabin, where the three men stood together. "Kit's nervous about everything," Chang continued, her voice lower. "But you…not so much. That coronal mass ejection took you by surprise, didn't it?"

"Not…they're not exactly rare, but, yes. One this early in the cycle, and such a big one. She took a breath. "But it was never out of the realm of possibilities."

Chang squinted at her. "Well, obviously, since it happened."

Elín shook her head. "I just meant…look, Jess, it's nothing to worry about," she said softly. "The Ring will protect us."

Chang nodded and pushed a lock of hair behind her ear. "Ok, brainiac. If you say so."

"Yes," said Elín. The Ring had survived many solar storms before.

They spoke no more about it, and the shutdown of Sector 32 was accomplished the same way as all the sectors before it. No more solar flares or coronal bursts, no more disrupted communications. All was quiet, everything proceeded as scheduled.

In Sector 32's control room, Elín sat at her post, watching the normal readings as they processed the shutdown procedure again.

"How's that residual magnetic interference from the CME earlier?" Bards asked. "Our comms have been working fine, but do we have long-range communications for our link with Command?"

"Everything's clear," said Elín.

"Ready to begin recording your report on your mark, sir," said Kit.

Bards recited the events of the day, and told Elín to report the stats of the CME; she gave a steady, direct data set, as Command would expect.

"Uplink is sending," said Kit, when they had finished the report. "And we're receiving the downlink from Command."

"Any personal messages in this download?" asked Timms, leaning over from his console to peer at Kit's screen.

Chang laughed. "Hoping for another dirty holo-vid from your girlfriend?"

"You wish, Chang."

Bards smiled. "We'll check the download when we get to the barracks in the next sector. Let's finish up here first."

Downlink files flashed across both Elín's and Kit's screens. As the files scrolled by, Elín spotted the urgent marker; she tapped at her console to pause the real-time view.

"Bards, there's a message marked urgent. It's from a Command Deep Space Telemetry Station."

Bards came to stand behind her chair, not quite touching her; warmth from his body pressed against her shoulders. "What is it, Halls?"

"It's a report from a long-range satellite at the outer edge of this solar system. As you all know, a long-period comet is passing through the inner solar system." Everyone had gathered around Elín's station while the downlink continued in real-time on Kit's screen. She read the report aloud anyway.

"The comet is still on its projected trajectory. It will be passing Epsilon Omega IV in fifteen standard hours at its projected distance of fifty million kilometers away. Even though the main body remains on course, the coronal mass ejection broke apart the dust tail and the ion tail. The tail has now been dispersed to twice its previous width, and the particles are scattering beyond the predicted range."

"What does that mean for us?" said Bards.

Elín shook her head. "There's a chance of minor impacts from the scattered cometary matter, but the particles are so small there's negligible chance of any damage." She glanced up at Bards. "The Telemetry Station just wanted to make us aware of the change to the comet's passage. It shouldn't interfere with our work."

"All right. Send an acknowledgement that we received the urgent message."

"Yes, sir," Elín said.

"Downlink complete," said Kit. "Data has been transferred to the portable storage unit."

"Timms, shut it down."

With the life support off, they walked through the dark empty corridors to the transport tubes. Despite their boots hitting the metal floor plates, their breathing filling the thinning air, the whisper of the transport tube's door and the hum of its motion, they left perfect stillness behind them. Elín leaned against a support pole and counted—nine more days to live in the growing silence of the Ring.

Below, the planet was beginning to exhale. Soon its icy breath would reach the Ring, but she would be long gone before the atmosphere swallowed what was left of her home.

STANDARD DAY CYCLE 9, 17:15 GST

The hours passed, tasks were checked off in order, and the sectors of the Ring died behind them, limbs severed from the whole. Inside the transport tube, the overhead light turned green, indicating the tube had stopped at Sector 28 and it was safe to exit. Elín stepped with the others out into the loading station.

Bards hit the door panel that led from the loading station into the rest of the sector. Nothing happened. He hit the panel again; it didn't light up, and the door didn't move.

"Huh," he said.

Chang rolled her eyes and flipped her hair back impatiently.

"Let me see it." Timms pulled a screwdriver off his tool belt and pried the panel cover off the wall. "Well. Okay, there's no power to these circuits. The door's completely dead." He reached inside the panel. "All right...hold on. Here's the manual switch."

With a clunk the door lock released and the door slid open a hand's width. Bards and Timms pulled it open the rest of the way. Dim red lighting and echoing silence greeted them.

"The life support is off," said Elín, almost to herself. The air clung to her skin with a stale chill, penetrating through the heavy fabric of her jumpsuit.

"Surely the clean-out crew wasn't stupid enough to shut it off when they left this sector," said Timms.

Bards shook his head. "That was definitely not part of their orders. Anyway, that would have been over a week ago."

"The system's only been off for a few hours," said Elín. "Otherwise the temperature would have dropped more."

"Come on, let's get to the control room," said Bards. They started walking.

"I bet that coronal mass ejection yesterday knocked out the power to this sector." Chang said.

"Not likely," said Bards. "This sector was in the full shadow of the planet at that time." He looked at Elín. "Right, Halls?"

She nodded. "That's right. And Kit and I took readings from each remaining sector; they all had power." Elín glanced at Kit just to make sure he agreed.

Kit nodded, his dark eyes wide beneath his shaggy bangs.

At the control room, Timms manually dragged open the door. Kit pulled a portable power module out of his pack and hooked it up to the main console. "Power and life support have been out in 28 for the past nine hours," he said. "And I'm not getting any readings from Sector 27..." he watched the screen another few seconds. "Nothing, sir."

"Do we not have enough power to link to the next sector's computers?" asked Bards.

"No," said Elín, leaning over Kit's shoulder and tapping a set of keys. "That's not the problem. Sector 27 is dead, just like this one. I can't tell if life support is running, but main power is down and computers are off-line."

"How did this happen?" said Bards, coming up beside Elín. "Kit, what's the status of solar activity?"

"Calm at the moment, sir," said Kit. "Magnetic and coronal activity is within normal parameters."

"Wait," said Elín. She usurped Kit's control of the console; sitting on the edge of his seat, she brought up a different view. "This is the planet." She touched the console screen lightly. Stable, even, blue waves crossed the graph, indicating acceptable planetary readings; a map of where everything was supposed to be. Red lines danced across the graph. They leapt higher and higher, taking erratic flight across the graph. They formed an entire new pattern of pulsing red, shifting away from what Epsilon Omega IV used to be.

"So...I'm guessing the red lines are bad?" said Chang.

"Very bad," whispered Kit.

"What are we looking at, Halls?" asked Bards.

Elín pointed at each shifting red line. "Upper atmospheric temperature, lower atmospheric temperature, core temperature. Rate of core rotation...all much higher than they should be." She tapped at more lines. "And these. Methane, helium, nitrogen, sulfur, ammonia—they're all thawing. Bards, the atmosphere is expanding. A lot faster than it should be."

"But that shouldn't have knocked out the power up here," said Bards. "Surely the atmosphere hasn't reached the Ring yet."

"The expanding outer layers of the atmosphere are still several thousand kilometers away," said Kit. "That's not the problem."

"It's the core rotation and the heat," said Elín. "It looks like the CME ignited a reaction in the mastotridium in the upper levels of the atmosphere. It's started a chain reaction—all the elements are heating up—the metals are falling to the center, and the core is spinning faster. The planet is developing a magnetosphere."

"But all of that is normal, right?" said Timms. "I mean, that's why we're shutting down the Array. The planetary core heats up, the magnetosphere grows, the Array gets fried."

"Except that wasn't supposed to even begin to happen for at least another ten to twenty years," said Bards.

Elín looked up at him. "Bards, if the planetary evolution continues at this rate, Epsilon Omega IV will have a fully developed magnetosphere, complete with poles, within months—not decades. This is only the beginning; all systems on the Ring Array will be non-functional long before that due to the proximity and force of the magnetic interference as the momentum increases."

"But we're out of here in less than a week," said Chang. She looked at Bards, then locked eyes with Elín. "Aren't we?"

"Kit," said Bards. "Is there any way to tell from here how many of the other sectors still have power or life support?"

Kit tapped at the console. "Sorry, sir. All I can see is what Halls said earlier—main power is down in Sector 27. We can't tell if life support is functioning, and I can't get any readings from any other sectors." He tapped again then shook his head. "I can't even look back to the sectors we just came from, besides 29."

"These portable units," muttered Timms, flicking at the power module Kit had plugged in to the computer. "They're weak as flashlights."

"It's not just the lack of power," said Elín. "Kit, look." She pointed at a series of green lines lying heavily at the bottom of the axis, silent. "Long-range comms are down. All comms are down."

Timms tapped his wrist-gear. "My comm still works."

"Right. We still have short-range," said Kit. "But without the comm boosters that are positioned throughout the Array," he pointed to a single green indicator, "our wrist-gear comms will probably barely reach from one end of a sector to the other."

"All right, I've seen enough," said Bards. "Let's go."

Kit unplugged the power unit and stood up, curling up the wire connectors. The glow from the console screen faded, leaving all their faces bathed in the eerie red emergency lighting.

"The transport tubes function on a dedicated source that's separate from the main power unit for each sector," said Elín, hurrying to keep stride beside Bards as he led them back down the corridor. "But as the magnetosphere grows, even that will be affected."

"I know." Bards looked at her and flashed a quick smile. "That's why we're cutting this party short. At full speed with no stops, the tube should have us back to Sector One in less than twelve hours."

Twelve hours. Elín felt a flutter of panic; she had wanted every second of the two weeks they'd been assigned so she could touch each part of the Ring just one more time. But in the next twelve hours, she would race past it all, every sector where people had once breathed, laughed, worked, and lived.

She felt cold as she boarded the tube. Chang stood beside her, grabbing the support pole above Elín's hand. Kit and Timms stood at another, and Bards stood alone at the controls at the front of the cabin.

"Get comfortable, people," said Bards. "It's going to be a long ride."

———————

STANDARD DAY CYCLE 9, 22:07 GST

"You know, Timms has the right idea," said Chang. "We should get some sleep."

Elín looked towards the far end of the cabin and saw Timms stretched out on his sleeping roll, his tool belt next to him. He was probably snoring quietly, but Elín couldn't hear it over the soft hum of the transport's drive. She and Chang were sitting on the floor with their backs against the smooth wall, their legs stretched out in front of them. Not far from where Timms was sleeping, Kit had rolled out his mat, but he was sitting up, studying his wrist-gear. Bards was sitting alone near the control console; his eyes were closed, but Elín knew he was awake.

"You're right." Elín glanced at her wrist-gear. "It's still a good seven hours before we get to Sector One."

"I'm glad to be leaving early," said Chang, reaching for her pack. "I feel like we've been stuck riding this hollow space-carousel forever."

Forever. Elín had always known that she wouldn't live here *forever*, or rather, for her entire life. She'd grown up here; then five years ago Command had revealed their plans to shut down the Ring. That decision had come six years after she and the other lead scientists onboard had determined that the planet was indeed entering its next phase of evolution. Even in the depths of the universe, all was constant motion. There was no forever.

Elín stuffed her food bar wrapper into her pack and began chewing the dissolvable dental gum they used to clean their teeth. She pulled out her sleeping mat, rolled it out on the floor, then looked back at Chang.

"Hey." Chang looked up from unpacking her sleeping roll. "I keep forgetting that you used to live here. I guess this place wasn't always this...spooky and useless, huh?

"Yeah." Elín tried to smile.

"Well, not too much longer now, and then we can move on to bigger and better things, right?" Chang unrolled her mat, and lay down on her stomach.

"Right...I guess so." Elín lay down and folded her hands on her chest. She felt Chang looking at her. She rolled her head and met Chang's eyes. "Goodnight, Jess."

Chang smiled and pillowed her head on her arm. "Night, Elín."

In her dream, Elín trembled. Like a slow redshift, everything was moving away, fading. Doppler lines trembled, the world trembled.

She snapped awake and held her breath. No, the trembling was real, not a dream. She looked around and saw Bards lying beside her. His dark eyes were wide, staring into hers.

"Did you feel that?" he whispered.

Elín nodded, and they both scrambled up. Kit was already standing at the control console at the front of the cabin. The floor was shaking, and the soft, familiar hum of the tube's drive had changed in pitch.

"Kit, what's happening?" asked Bards.

Kit glanced at Bards and then Elín as they came to stand beside him. "Not...exactly sure," he said. "Our speed has slowed by almost four percent, but I'm not registering a problem with the drive." He nodded at the console screen.

"Is it something with the tube shaft itself?" asked Bards.

"I don't think so...sir," said Kit. "None of the standard alerts have been initiated."

"It's the comet," said Elín. She punched at the console, but of course, nothing happened—the computers were down in every sector, so they had nothing to link to and no external sensors.

"What's going on?" asked Chang. Elín glanced over to see her and Timms rising from their mats.

"Interference from the comet...we think," said Bards. "That message from the Deep Space Telemetry Station said there was a chance of minor impacts from the scattered dust tail."

Elín checked the time on her wrist-gear. "We're just at the right position to be catching the edge of it."

"But it's just dust particles—gases, little tiny meteors, right?" said Timms. "How is that enough to cause damage to the inside of the transport tube?"

"Well, technically, there's no damage," said Kit. "We've just dropped four percent in speed and efficiency."

"That's probably due to interference from the scattered ion tail more than the dust," said Elín. "Remember, we're on the tube that runs along the inner top edge of the Ring—that's the one the clean-out crew left operating. If we were on one of the interior tracks we'd have more of the Ring around us and we probably wouldn't notice a thing."

Bards looked at Kit and then Elín. "Aside from the slight drop in speed, do you anticipate any other problems or interference? Do we need to disembark at the next station?"

Kit frowned over the console again. "Not according to any of these indicators, sir, but they're...we're...limited."

Elín nodded. "I agree. I don't think we're in any danger, Bards."

"All right. We'll sit tight, then; just a little longer ride back."

"That's fine with me," said Timms, going back over to his mat. "I really didn't want to spend the next few days walking back to Sector One."

Chang went back to her mat and lay on her back with her arms crossed above her head. After a moment, Kit left the control console and returned to his mat. Elín stayed at the console with Bards.

He met her eyes and gave her a little smile. "Everything's fine, Halls."

"I know." The trembling had stopped, but the hum of the transport drive was still lower, shifted into a longer wavelength—so slight, but so apparent. Redshift.

Elín moved away from Bards and lay back down on her mat. Sleep felt far away. She forced her eyes closed and hoped for no dreams.

Chapter 3

———

Sector One was cold and silent. Breath formed in filmy clouds around the five of them as they walked. White beams from their flashlights cut through the red dimness.

Their cargo ship lay waiting, docked and quiet. Bards and Timms had to manually wrestle open the airlock. The moment she stepped through the airlock into the ship's loading bay, Elín knew. They would not be leaving the Ring behind just yet.

"Something's wrong," she said. Chang pushed past her.

"What do you mean, Halls?" asked Bards. He gave a grunt as he and Timms slid the ship's airlock hatch back into place.

"We have no power—that's what's wrong." Chang's voice came from down the corridor. "The ship's life support has been in standby mode, and I think that's still working. But all main power is offline. That means no engines."

Elín went to join Chang in the cockpit. Every console was dark. Chang punched at the engine controls and no reaction came. She ran her fingers up the dead keyboard, looked at Elín, and tossed up her hands.

Bards came into the cockpit. "No power and no engines? That's an awful lot of ugly from a dissipated comet tail. What else could be affecting these systems?"

"I'll find out, sir," Elín answered, sliding the pack off her back and digging for her portable power module. "And someone should go check out the engine room."

Bards nodded. "Chang, Timms, go check the engines."

Timms had just appeared in the cockpit doorway; he nodded and headed back down the corridor with Chang close behind. Kit came into the cockpit and pulled out his power module.

The pilot's console hummed to life as Elín plugged in; Kit sat next to her and started up the copilot's console.

"Life support is still on standby," said Kit. "Bringing it up to full power."

The sigh of the air recyclers filled the small space of the cockpit, and the primary lighting came on, lifting the sickly red pallor cast by the emergency lights.

"Good job, Kit," said Bards. He came and stood between the live stations. "Halls...is that what I think it is?"

"I'm afraid so, sir." Elín turned from her screen to look up at Bards. Tiny lines of worry creased around his dark eyes as he squinted at the screen. She pulled her eyes away to look back at the console. "There's a hull breach in one of the secondary engine compartments and one of the cargo bays. And the starboard engine nacelle has been damaged."

Bards' wrist-gear beeped. "I hate to be the bearer of bad news, Bards," came Timms' voice through bursts of static. "But we're in bad shape down here. The port engine can be patched up pretty easily, but the starboard engine needs major work."

"That's not all. A lot of the circuits have been overloaded, too," came Chang's voice. "Fried by an energy surge, looks like."

"She's got a hull breach, as well," said Bards.

"Damn," said Timms. "How the hell did this happen?"

"I've got some of the external sensors working now; our ship was on the sunward side of the planet when the CME blast hit," said Elín, bringing up an animated graphic of the ring on her console. "My guess is some larger particles from the dust tail were affected by the force of the event and impacted the ship. It looks like two of the docked exo-pods dislodged from their clamps; one of them must have hit the starboard nacelle and that section of the hull."

More static came from Bards' wrist-gear. "Um, sir?" said Chang. "If we're going to get this ship moving at all, we're going to have to fix that nacelle from the outside. Somebody's got to go EVA."

"More than one somebody, more like," added Timms.

Elín tapped at her console. "He's right, Bards. If we were docked at a functioning repair station..." But they weren't. No such thing existed on the Ring anymore.

"Are we in danger of comet debris out there?" asked Bards.

"We've rotated out of the main path of the comet's debris," said Elín. "But because the tail got scattered by the CME there's still a chance we could encounter a particle cloud."

Bards sighed and looked out the cockpit window. "All right. Kit, you're on sensor duty—I want those sensors working well enough to tell me if any comet debris is headed our way. You are looking for anything...*anything* that could endanger EVA workers. I'll man the tether controls. Halls, Timms, Chang—suit up and head outside."

STANDARD DAY CYCLE 10, 10:18 GST

Elín's shadow crawled ahead of her along the outer hull of the ship, a sharp edged blackness in the glow from the planet behind her. She hadn't been outside the Ring in a suit in many years; and the feeling was terrifying and exhilarating. She could see her planet from any window, but out here, with nothing between them, she could tell that that Epsilon Omega IV was nearer than before. Warming clouds raced outwards; and invisible, but much closer, were the thrashing bands of the growing magnetosphere.

Her comm cracked with static. "We've got the replacement relays installed, *finally*," came Chang's voice. "We're set to attempt a power link. You ready, Halls?"

"Almost there," Elín replied. She gave a small grunt as she tugged at the access hatch covering the secondary power cables. As the panel popped open, the force of her pull sent her floating backwards away from the ship; she kept a grip on the edge of the hatch door and pulled herself back against the hull. Her tether drifted and swirled behind her. She pulled an ion-spanner from her belt and plunged it into the access port inside the hatch. "All right, Chang, I'm ready."

"Okay—on my mark. Three, two, one, mark."

Elín twisted the spanner in the socket. A faint shudder went through the hull, the sensation translating through her padded EVA suit.

"I think that's got it," said Chang. "I've got forty percent power here now. Timms, what do you show?"

"Still under ten percent for this conduit," said Timms. "But let me check the auxiliary one. Bards, can you give me a little more line?"

"On it," came Bards' voice. "You've got two more meters of tether."

"That should do it," said Timms. "Okay, Chang. I've got twelve percent over here at the auxiliary port."

"Crap," said Chang. "All right, people. Looks like we've got some more tinkering to do."

"I'll be right there," said Elín. She closed the hatch and returned the tool to her belt pouch. She gave herself a gentle push and skimmed along the skin of the ship back towards the starboard nacelle.

"Sir!" came Kit's voice over the comm, through a burst of static. "I'm picking up more solar flare activity."

"Will it interfere with their work out there?" Bards asked.

"No, but—" Static hissed through Kit's voice.

"Say again, Kit?" said Elín. There was a pause, with only static. "Bards, can you read me?"

"I read you, Halls; stand by. Kit?"

"...sol...flares are interf...communic...," came Kit's voice, broken and thick with static. "Sir...been...anoth...coronal mass eject..."

Elín paused in her crawling, hanging onto an exo-pod clamp port to halt her forward movement. The reflected glow of the planet was still behind her, but ahead beyond the ship she could see the edge of the Ring, disappearing into the distance. Sunlight crept along the top of the Ring, encroaching on the blue penumbra where they rested.

Kit's transmission cleared. "We're going to be out in full sun in sixteen minutes," he said. "The leading edge of the CME's radiation shockwave will hit us in approximately twenty-five minutes. The first wave of plasma...about thirty minutes."

"Everybody back inside now," said Bards.

"But, we're almost done with this," said Timms.

"It can wait," said Bards.

"No, sir, it can't," Chang's voice interrupted him. "We've got too many exposed components here. If a blast of radiation and plasma hits this nacelle in its current state, there won't be enough left of it for us to repair."

Another flare of static. "...right," Bards' voice crackled. "...fifteen minutes."

Elín changed direction, crawling swiftly back the way she'd come. "Bards, I need more line. I'm going to help them."

"Halls—"

"Fifteen minutes—I know, sir."

Elín heard his sigh through the static. "You have five...meters."

"Thank you, sir."

Chang and Timms clung to opposite ends of the nacelle. Chang beckoned to Elín. "Give Timms a hand with the hull plating," she said over the comm. "I'm working on this section."

Elín crawled up beside Timms. He was fastening a sheet of plating over an exposed section of the nacelle. They had stripped a piece of plating from the breached cargo bay, so the shape and size were wrong, but it would suffice. Several sections of hull plating had been sheared away by cometary debris and the impact from the dislodged exo-pod.

"We've got to get this covered as best as we can," said Timms. "You get this corner down while I screw down this side."

Elín pulled a hammer from her belt pouch. The silent blow of the hammer sent a shudder up her arm. Together, slowly, they bent the plating enough to cover the innards of the nacelle. Elín held the sheet of hull in place and Timms twisted his screwdriver.

"Two minutes." Bards' voice came through a burst of static.

"Yes, sir," said Elín.

"Aaand...got it," said Chang. She pushed away from the nacelle, heading for an exhaust port at the back of the ship.

Blue-white sunlight bathed them in brightness. Even dead, the Ring continued its steady rotation, smooth and unchanging. Elín squinted towards the Epsilon Omega star. An ethereal haze of light hung between the planet and the star—the wave of superheated stellar plasma, racing through the solar system.

"I'm getting another reading," came Kit's voice. "There's a sizable debris cloud heading your way. It's hard to tell with all the interference coming from the planet, but—"

"Back inside—all of you," Bards interrupted. "Now."

"Almost done," said Chang.

A wisp of fine, reflective dust, so faint it could have been an illusion, skittered across the hull in front of Elín; like a ghost, barely glittering in the sunlight, dust particles streamed past.

"Your sensors are reading it right, Kit," said Elín.

"Damn, that was a big piece," said Timms. "Half the size of my hand! It just missed the hull. Bards, if a rock that size hits this nacelle again, these patches might not hold."

"Then we'll fix it again after the dust cloud's gone and the CME is past," said Bards. "I'm pulling you in."

"Wait...not yet," said Chang.

Elín pulled herself along her tether towards the airlock, and watched the line grow shorter as Bards reeled it in. More dust particles danced past, bigger flakes this time, almost the size of her fingernails. At the speed the particles were traveling, if one of them was sharp enough to pierce her suit...

"Chang!" shouted Timms.

Elín snapped her head around. Chang had drifted out from the ship, her line taut as Bards reeled her in, and she hung there, surrounded by a swirling cloud of silvery particles. Four tiny, white bursts of air sprayed out from her body as she writhed in the cloud.

"Her suit's been breached!" Elín shouted. She pushed away from the ship towards Chang's line, stretching her arms out to reach her. More dust streamed past her gloves, and she felt a sudden jolt as air escaped from between her fingers.

Squeezing her hand into a fist to seal the breach, Elín grabbed Chang's line with her other hand and pulled.

"The tether reel is at full speed," said Bards' voice.

Elín felt the two lines tugging at her in opposing directions. Chang hung at the end of her tether, compressed air hissing silently at Elín and pushing her away. Elín pulled at the line, and as Chang drew closer, she saw more of the fist-sized debris. Before she could shout, a chunk of rock slammed into the line, and it snapped.

"Chang!"

"Oh, my God!" said Timms. "Bards! Let the line out—we've got to get her!"

With the inertia from the air leaks, Chang's body hurtled away from them. There was no answer on her comm to their shouts.

Not again. This could not happen again. All it had taken was a snapped line, and her father had never come back home. Elín kicked frantically at the airless vacuum around her. "Let out our lines, Bards!"

"Oh, God," said Timms' voice. "Bards, the miner—"

The pitted hull of a mining array flashed through the clouds of the planet. Chang's body, growing rapidly smaller against the backdrop of the sky below, was on a perfect collision trajectory.

"Chang, no!" Elín unfisted her hand, holding it behind her, and let the escaping air push her away from the ship and the Ring. Too little; not fast enough.

"Halls has a suit breach, too!" she heard Timms' voice. "Reel us in faster, Bards!"

The line was tugging Elín back towards the Ring. *Jess!* She thrashed against the line.

"Got you!" Timms' voice sounded in her headset and she felt him grab her arm.

"No!"

"I'm pulling you both in," said Bards. "Brace for re-entry."

Elín struggled against Timms' hold, but suddenly her entire body was slammed with gravity and her movement turned into a feeble protest. She felt the floor shake as the hatch door slammed shut behind them.

"Sir..." came Kit's voice over the speaker in the airlock. Elín pulled away from Timms as he took off her helmet for her.

Silence fell over the comm. Elín stood frozen with her tether loose in her hands. Timms jabbed the door panel, and the door into the airlock control room slid open.

Bards was standing at the main console, one hand still on the tether controls, his other hand raised as he shouted into his wrist-gear. "Kit! Report!"

"Chang has collided with the mining equipment." Kit's voice was a whisper. "Continued trajectory towards the planet. The miner is also off-course—predicted orbital decay within minutes. Chang will reach the ammonia layer of the upper atmosphere in ten seconds. The atmospheric friction..." His voice trailed off into silence.

"You killed her!" Elín hurled herself into the control room and swung a fist at Bards. She missed his head and her punch slammed into a monitor; she heard the bone in her hand crack even through the padded gloves of her suit. No pain—just the hollowness of betrayal, as her beautiful Epsilon Omega IV claimed another soul.

"You didn't pull her in fast enough!" Elín hurled her arm again, and Bards caught her wrist.

"Stand down, Halls!"

"I think I'm...I'm going to be sick." Timms' voice was slurred. He staggered past Bards and retched into a trash receptacle.

Elín twisted her arm against Bards' grip, and then gave a yelp of pain. Bards released her.

"Come on." Bards' voice was quiet. "Let's get you both to the infirmary."

STANDARD DAY CYCLE 10, 21:02 GST

Everything had shifted. The Ring was dying, and it had taken another human soul with it. Quiet, cold Epsilon Omega IV was alive with heat, and the birthing pangs of its metamorphosis battered the Ring, the ship, and now its inhabitants. The long-range communications relays stayed smothered, mute.

Elín shut off the console and leaned her head against the bulkhead by the cockpit window. In the distance, the Epsilon Omega star was bright blue; calm and indifferent again.

"Halls. There you are." Bards' voice from the doorway. Elín didn't turn around. She heard his footsteps as he came into the cockpit and closed the distance between them.

"What do you want, Bards?"

"It's past time for our sleep cycle."

"I'm not tired." Her healing hand still ached, but the pain was not enough to keep her from sleeping. She wished it were. "I've been trying to get the long-range communications online, but..."

"You need rest. It's been a hard day, for all of us."

Elín spun to face him. He had come up right behind her, his face close, unreadable. She raised her good arm; her right hand was still wrapped in a cocoon of bandages while the bone-mending implant finished its work. Bards caught her wrist.

"It's been a hard day?" she echoed. "A hard day? Jess is dead!" She jerked her arm against Bards' grip, but he held on. "You killed her!"

"Halls—"

Elín felt her heart rate rising. Why wouldn't the tears come? There were tears when her father fell. She hadn't been there, hadn't seen him.... But she'd had Jess's tether; she *had* her.

Bards released her wrist and slid his hand to rest on her shoulder. Elín let her arm fall to her side as she stared into his dark eyes. "I killed her, Bards."

He shook his head.

"I killed her!" Elín heard her voice cracking. "I let her go! I saw the rock coming, I didn't pull her in fast enough! I could have saved her."

"Halls, you know this was not your fault." Bards gripped her upper arms, his hands tight.

Elín tried to back away from him, but he moved with her as she stepped backwards. "Don't you dare tell me that it was no one's fault!" She shook her head. "Don't you dare say it was an accident! Someone's got to take the blame for this—I had her line!"

"No, *I* had her line!" Bards' sudden shout startled her. "You were all on my line—I was at the controls. I ordered you out there. I'm in command, the blame is on me!"

"You're pulling rank at a time like this?" Elín twisted her arms in his grip, but he didn't let go. "This has nothing to do with you! My planet killed her! This is *my* home, I let it—"

"Shut up, Halls! Shut up!" Bards pushed her up against the wall, his hands still gripping her arms. "This *was* your home. Now it's time for it to die, and it's my job to make sure my people don't die with it!"

"Jess is dead!"

"I know that!" His breath was hot on her face; his normally smooth features twisted with anger. "She's gone. Jess is gone and it's my fault...mine! Not *yours...not—*"

Her cheeks burned as the tears finally burst forth, washing away her sight, taking her voice from her. "No..." She choked on her words.

Bards still gripped her arms; he pressed his body into her, pinning her to the wall. She tasted her tears as he crushed his lips against hers.

The kiss was hard and desperate, a gravity well she couldn't fight. A blueshift; heartbeats quickening as they moved together. Bards held her until Elín could barely breathe anymore, and still he held their kiss. She gripped his jumpsuit with her good hand and held on tight.

Finally he broke away, but his lips stayed close enough to brush against hers as he spoke. "No one else is going to die, Halls."

You're wrong, Solomon. The whole world is dying. She tightened her fist around the fabric of his jumpsuit.

"Do you trust me, Halls?"

His voice was a whisper. She wanted to swallow his whisper with her mouth and never speak again, never think again.

"Elín, do you trust me?"

She moved her eyes up to meet his. "Yes; with my life."

His hands were no longer gripping her arms, but were cradling her body. Instead of the cold wall at her back, she felt his strong hands moving across her shoulder blades, down her spine.

"Come on," Bards said quietly. "It's late, and we have a lot of work to do tomorrow." His arms released her. Redshift.

Elín went with him out of the room. They walked in silence down the corridor towards the sleeping quarters. She wanted to touch him again, but was afraid he might move out of reach if she did.

Chapter 4

Standard Day Cycle 11, 08:44 GST

Bards folded his arms across his chest, and looked at each one of them in turn—first Timms, then Kit, and his eyes lingered on Elín. "All right. What are our options?"

"The engines still aren't working," said Timms, rubbing at his beard. "I might be able get the port side up and running—that's the one that was just overloaded by the radiation. But the starboard engine...I don't know." He shook his head. "Most of the repairs we did yesterday were trashed by the CME blast and all that...debris. I'll have to go EVA again to make absolutely sure, but...I don't know if it's possible to get that engine working again at all."

"It is possible to fly the ship with just the one engine, but what are our other limitations?" asked Bards.

"Well, once I get the port engine working, I can reroute the power. It'll be slow going, and might be a bumpy ride. The inertial compensators are specifically designed for each engine, so combining the power..." Timms trailed off and glanced at Elín. "It'll take some finagling but I can get us moving."

"We also have the maneuvering jets," said Elín. "It's a simpler system, so there were fewer circuits to be fried by the CME. I can have most of the jets working again in a few hours."

Bards nodded. "Communications?"

Elín shook her head and looked at Kit.

"At this point, we're lucky our wrist-gear comms are working, sir," he said. "The magnetic interference coming from the planet is increasing—plus, the sun is still very active. All of the comm boosters positioned on the Ring are useless, as we discovered while we were there. Then after yesterday's CME...." He looked at the floor, but then straightened back up. "There is a...there's a deep space comm relay in orbit around the largest moon. It's far enough away from the planet that it shouldn't have been affected by the growing magnetosphere; not yet, anyway. And it was designed to withstand intense solar activity, so if the dust tail didn't strike it..."

"So if we get the engines working and get out to the moon, we could get a message to Command," said Bards.

"Yeah, but why bother at that point?" said Timms. "The hyper-driver transport is in orbit around the moon." He looked at Kit, and then Elín. "It's parked near that moon, right? Or is it a different one?"

"It's that moon, Melpomene," said Elín. "The hyper-driver is in a Lagrangian point orbit between the planet and Melpomene."

"Are we sure that the driver transport is undamaged?" Bards asked.

There was silence.

"There's no way to tell, sir," said Kit finally, "without the long-range sensors. I...I'm assuming that the deep space comm relay is still intact, so therefore the driver transport should be as well...that's my best guess." He furrowed his eyebrows.

"Right, Kit. Except the comm relay is designed to withstand volatile solar storms," said Bards. "But the driver transport was not. And then there's the scattered cometary tails; we lost an exo-pod."

"The driver transport flies through hyper-space," said Timms. "Surely it can stand up to some radiation."

"Radiation within the hyper-space dimension is not at all the same thing as radiation and solar plasma from a B-type star," Elín said, frowning at him.

Timms gave her a mild glare. "I know that. I just meant—"

"It doesn't matter," Bards interrupted him. "The point is, we can't stay here. We need those engines working now."

"Yes, sir," said Timms.

"All right, people. Let's get to work."

———

STANDARD DAY CYCLE 11, 15:51 GST

After seven hours, the ship still had nothing but the maneuvering jets. Elín bit into a food bar and stared at the tangle of ruptured conduits overhead; the spilled guts of a mortal wound. From deeper inside the engine cavity, she could hear the hissing whine of the plasma fuser. The sound stopped, and Timms' voice muttered a curse.

"Is everything okay?" Elín called, looking up into the crawl space.

"No," said Timms. "Only two of the fuel injectors aren't completely wrecked. Even with this fuser, I don't think I can get this third conduit into a safely usable state. Better tell Bards that we'll be stuck for a while longer."

Elín went over to the doorway that led into the engine control room; Kit was standing at a console. His dark, narrow eyes were tight with worry.

"There's still no power to the engines," he said, turning to look at Elín.

"I know. Timms is having trouble with the fuel injector conduits. Where's Bards?"

"Right here." Bards stepped into the control room. "Still a no-go?"

"I'm afraid so, sir," said Elín. "All we have are the directional jets; they aren't enough to move us far or fast, but..."

"Well, that's something." Bards came towards the doorway; Elín stepped back to let him in. His body filled the doorway and all of her senses as he looked up into the engine cavity; she felt herself blush and she looked away. "Timms," he said. "What's it looking like in there?"

"It's looking like we can't get this bucket running without some actual replacement parts," Timms called down.

"Not going to happen."

"Don't I know it, sir."

"Maybe there is something..." said Elín.

Bards lifted an eyebrow at her. "Halls?"

"All you need is a fuel injector conduit; right, Timms?"

Timms' head appeared above them as he leaned out of the engine cavity. He pushed his protective lenses up onto the top of his head. "Well, I wouldn't say that's *all* we need, but, yeah, it's the main thing. And it's the one thing that's too badly damaged to even patch up."

"The life support system in the Ring uses conduits similar to these. One of the smaller sizes might fit."

Bards looked at Elín, then up at Timms. "What do you think?"

Timms nodded. "It's worth a shot. We're not going anywhere with what we've got right now."

"The Ring's life support has been off for days," Elín said. "There's more than enough breathable air, but the temperature will have dropped considerably."

"The thermal lining in the EVA suits should keep you warm enough for a few hours," said Bards. He looked at Elín, lifting his eyebrows again.

She nodded.

"All right. Timms, you and Halls go get those conduits—and anything else you see that we might need."

Timms swung down out of the engine cavity and clambered down the ladder rungs on the wall. "Will do, Bards," he said.

Bards nodded at him, and then looked back at Elín. He didn't smile, but his eyes were soft. Elín held his gaze, and wished that she never had to look away again. "Good luck," Bards said finally. "And be careful."

―――――――――

STANDARD DAY CYCLE 11, 19:23 GST

They were in an auxiliary maintenance control room in the Ring, the nearest one to where their ship was docked. Like the rest of the Ring, this room was dark, lit only with the red glow of emergency lights. The still air chilled Elín even through the thermal layer. Her right hand ached. With fingers numb inside her gloves, she loaded conduit pieces and circuit casings onto a supply cart.

Timms' arm appeared from the access hatch in the wall, holding out the end of another conduit tube. Elín took the end from him and pulled it the rest of the way out of the hatch. Her stiff fingers lost their grip as the tube caught; it fell to the floor with a slow bounce in the light gravity.

"It's snagged on something in there," said Elín, bending to pick up the end of the tube.

Timms leaned back into the hatch, adjusting the flashlight clamped to his chest. "I see it. Hang on. Okay—try now."

Elín pulled again, and the tube slithered out of the hatch, coiling slowly on the floor. She gathered it up and stuffed it into the cart.

"I think that should do it." Timms' breath was a burst of fog in the stale air. "If these don't work, nothing will."

"We'll make it work," said Elín. They had to.

Timms climbed out of the hatch and they began the long walk back to the docking port. The vast emptiness of the Ring seemed to swallow their footsteps and the hum of the cart's wheels. Emergency lights illuminated a dusky path for them down a corridor with windows.

Elín didn't want to look, but the edge of the planet was just visible, its reflected glow bathing them in light as they walked. The blue clouds were turning white with heat. The expanding atmosphere looked almost close enough to touch now. Somewhere in those roiling toxic clouds floated Chang, and her father. *I don't want to leave you here.* They turned from the windowed corridor and were plunged into red dimness again.

When she and Timms finally reached the airlock to their ship, he punched at the control panel and the door slid open. Elín laid her hand on the wall, letting the cold metal penetrate through her glove. *Thank you.* As a final tribute to the life it had supported for so long, the Ring was able to give this one last gift.

Timms glanced over his shoulder at her as he pushed the cart through the door. "Hey, you okay, Halls?"

She pulled her hand away from the wall. "I'm fine."

Back in the warm air of the ship, Elín stripped off her thermal layer and joined Timms in the engine room. She scrambled up and down and up the rungs of the ladder, bringing him parts and tools.

"That's it. The conduit's fused," Timms called down to her from the engine cavity. "Have Kit check the readings again."

Elín leaned backwards from the ladder, keeping hold of one of the rungs. "Kit!" she called. "What's it look like now?"

There was a pause, then Bards appeared in the doorway. "Kit says it's at thirty-seven percent."

Elín sighed and looked up at the opening above her head. "Thirty-seven percent, Timms."

"Oh for.... All right, all right—hand me another one of those tubing sockets."

Bards looked up at Elín as she climbed up the ladder with the socket in hand. "What's your progress?"

Timms stuck his head out of the ceiling cavity as he reached for the socket. "Not much, if we're only at thirty-seven percent. I'm sorry, Bards—I really had hoped to have this thing working by now. The damage is more extensive than I'd originally thought, and trying to reroute the power so that the ship can function with just the one engine..."

"It's not your fault, Timms. Just keep working. In the meantime, I'm going to fly out to the deep space comm array."

"What?" said Timms.

Elín closed her eyes and said nothing.

"We can't stay here much longer," said Bards. "The planet is becoming more and more unstable. And we still don't know if the hyper-driver transport is even usable. A distress call to Command is our best shot."

"But how are you—" began Timms.

Elín climbed back down the ladder. "An exo-pod. Bards, are you sure that's a good idea? We have only two pods left, and we haven't checked them for damage. And what about fuel levels? They're only meant to circle the ring and dock."

"One of them has minor hull damage, but the other one looks okay. Halls, I want you to double-check it to make sure it's travel-worthy, then transfer the fuel cell out of the other one. If we combine the tanks from both and if I time my launch for when this part of the Ring comes around to the moon it will be enough to get out there. I already had Kit run the numbers."

"But—" said Timms again.

Bards held up a hand. "Timms, I'm not doubting your and Halls' ability to get the ship going. But we're running out of time."

Timms gave an exaggerated sigh, and withdrew up into the engine cavity.

"But if we're not able to get the engines working, how will we come get you?" said Elín. "It'll take you at least twenty hours to get to Melpomene. Will you have enough fuel and life support to make it back to us?"

"I'll wear a suit inside the pod to supplement the life support. And there will be enough fuel." His dark face was serious, his eyes intense. "I've already started emptying the salvage out of the pod. Just make sure it can get me out to the comm relay, Halls."

She swallowed and looked him in the eyes. "Yes, sir."

His face softened. "You're in command while I'm gone. Keep these guys in line." The hint of a smile. "Wish me luck, Halls."

"Yes, sir." *Good luck, Solomon.* She reached out to touch him, but just brushed his sleeve. "We'll get the ship moving. We'll come for you, Bards."

Chapter 5

Standard Day Cycle 12, 23:11 GST

The Ring turned, as it always had, and spun them into the darkness behind the planet. The moon was far away now, and somewhere in that expanse, Bards was all alone.

Her own breath was the only sound. Elín had ordered Timms and Kit to take three hours of rest. They had all worked well past the sleep cycle. She closed her eyes and leaned her head back against the headrest of the copilot's seat. She wished she could dream, though she feared what dreams might come.

She slept lightly, and at the three-hour alarm she woke the men, and they began to work again. So close now. Elín pulled the protective lenses over her face and gripped a conduit with gloved hands. Her arms trembled from holding the shuddering tube, and her back ached from her hunched position inside the engine cavity, but she kept still.

Timms shut off the fuser. "That's got it. Check it now."

Elín released the conduit and rubbed at her aching arms. She leaned her head down through the opening into the engine room below. "Kit! What are our numbers?"

"Eighty-nine point five!"

"What'd he say?" asked Timms; he was above Elín, deeper in the engine.

"Eighty-nine point five," she said, pushing her lenses up onto her forehead so she could look at him properly. "I say we try it with that. What do you think?"

Timms nodded. "I agree. I doubt we're going to get much more than that. Let's do it."

They gathered up their tools and climbed down out of the engine. Timms closed and latched the cavity shielding. Elín pulled off her gloves as she went into the engine control room.

"We're going to go with the eighty-nine percent," she said to Kit. "Timms, you take the controls in here. Kit, you're with me in the cockpit."

Elín kept the comm open with Timms as she ran through the launch procedure. "Power on, start-up sequence initiated. Maneuvering jets online."

"Engine holding, inertial compensators online," Timms reported back.

"Releasing docking clamps." A shudder went through the ship. "Jets active. Departing the Ring port."

As the ship moved away, the view of the Ring and its planet expanded through the window. This was the first time in years that she had left the Ring. Out here, she could see the Ring Array for what it was—a man-made triumph, completing a purposeful life, now surrendering in the arms of the universe that bore its creators. *Goodbye.*

"Setting a course for Melpomene," Elín said. She looked over at Kit and he gave her a nod of confirmation. She turned the jet controls until the ship's position matched the coordinates Kit had programmed into the flight computer. "Engines go."

With another mighty shudder the ship began to move. No alarms flashed.

"We're at one-third throttle, Timms," she said into the comm. "How's it looking in there?"

"So far so good. All the conduits are holding, and there's even fuel injection. Give it some more power."

Elín eased the controls up. "One-half now. Two-thirds."

The ship began to shake, as the port inertial compensator struggled to accommodate the missing starboard one. But no engine alarms sounded, and their speed and course remained steady. "I'm giving it full power," Elín said.

Because of the single engine, even their full speed was slow, but they were moving. And they were moving much faster than an exo-pod.

"Start scanning with everything you've got," she said to Kit. "It's been almost nineteen hours—Bards should be near the comm relay soon, maybe even heading back."

"Yes, ma'am."

The magnetic interference from Epsilon Omega IV still kept their comms and sensors smothered, but Elín hoped that the farther away from the planet they got, the less they would be affected.

The ride was bumpy, as Timms had predicted, and Elín felt the periodic disconcerting shifts in gravity. The space ahead of them lay featureless, with no sign of Bards; the long-range sensors still blind.

The comm flared to life with a burst of static. "...Bards...read me?"

Elín lurched forward and slammed her hand on the comm button. "Bards! We read you!"

Another flare of static. "...not sure...reading me. Message...Command.   Hyper...damaged...fuel...orbit around...copy?"

"Bards, we're reading you! Say again?" Elín looked at Kit. "Can you boost the signal?"

He shook his head. "I'm doing everything I can. I think the only reason he's getting through at all is because he's at the comm relay. We can hear, but I don't know if our signal is clear enough to carry a reply."

"Bards, we're coming." She tried not to shout into the comm. She checked the flight console. "Our ETA is two hours. Just hold on."

Only static.

Elín switched to the internal comm. "Timms, any chance we could go faster?"

"Well, everything's holding together," his voice replied. "But power output is at safe maximum. I wouldn't try anything more than two or three percent."

Three percent was better than nothing. "I'll bring it up slowly," Elín said. "Half a percent at a time." She laid a gentle finger on the controls.

An alarm sounded as she nudged the engines to three percent above safe maximum, so she eased it back down to two. "How are we, Timms?"

"We're in one piece, mostly. Just don't do that again; it could cause an engine shutdown. Looks like two percent over maximum is all we can get."

Elín released the controls and slumped back in her seat. ETA to the moon was down to an hour and fifty-four minutes. *We're coming, Solomon.*

─────────

STANDARD DAY CYCLE 13, 00:26 GST

Forty minutes away from the moon, several of the long-range sensors came to life. Elín and Kit worked the controls in tandem, recalibrating, concentrating, silently hoping. Nothing was at full power or full range, but the magnetic disturbances from the planet were fainter out here, slowly resigning their hold.

She could get clear readings on the planet again, and they were startling. Heat and core rotation had increased exponentially since the last time she'd been able to read a complete scan. Magnetism off the scale, the magnetosphere forming far more rapidly than initial data had projected. Epsilon Omega IV was an entirely new creature.

"No sign of the hyper-driver transport so far," said Kit. "Still trying to compensate..." He adjusted more controls. "Even with our impaired sensors, at this distance we should be getting a reading from it. It must have been damaged—I'm not picking up a homing signal or any power output, even in a standby mode."

"What about the exo-pod?"

"Still scanning...there's still a lot of interference." Kit made minute adjustments to his controls, tilting his head.

Elín opened the comm. "Bards, do you read me? Bards, this is Halls—please respond." She took a breath. "We're forty minutes away from the moon. What is your position?"

Only silence answered.

She looked at Kit. "Aren't we close enough to the comm relay to get a signal out?"

"Theoretically, but I'm picking up more electromagnetic interference and...oh, God."

"What?" Elín looked hard at him, then down at the console. *No.*

"Timms," she called into the comm. "If there's anything you can do to get us more speed, now's the time. We're forty minutes away, and we need to be there in less than thirty."

"I already told you, Halls, we're at...oh, hell! You've got to be kidding."

"More speed, Timms," Elín snapped, and then switched the comm back to external. "Bards, if you can hear me, if you have any fuel left, you've got to get into the penumbra of the moon. There's another CME coming."

"Still no sign of the pod," said Kit.

Damn you, Solomon, where are you? "Keep scanning, Kit. And keep sending a beacon with our ship ID. Even if he can't hear an audio transmission, maybe he can pick up on that."

Kit gave a tight nod.

"All right down there, give her a nudge," came Timms' voice. "Half a percent at a time...*slowly*."

Gradually, painfully, the ship's speed increased. An engine warning alarm sounded, and Elín shut it off. ETA to Melpomene, thirty-three minutes; front end of the radiation wave from the sun, twenty-six minutes. Elín eased the controls higher.

The dark gray moon filled the window. Elín finally spotted the circular frame of the hyper-driver transport in the distance, off course from where it was supposed to be parked, signal lights dark. They wouldn't be leaving that way.

The ship lurched and another alarm sounded.

"Engines are down!" called Timms. "Ruptured conduits and overloaded circuits. I'm sorry, Halls, but that's it. We're floating dead. Maybe if I had—"

"You did what you could, Timms," Elín cut him off. "Our inertia and maneuvering jets will have to take us from here."

"Outer hull is heating up," said Kit. "Radiation rising. The shielding will protect us from the radiation, but once the plasma wave gets here..."

"I know," said Elín. The ship groaned around them. She clenched her teeth and pushed full power to the jets, and they crawled into the shadow of the moon.

"I see the pod!" cried Kit. "A thousand kilometers away, just a few thousand meters above the surface of the moon. It looks like he was in a low orbit, but it's decaying rapidly."

Elín hit the comm button again. "Bards! Answer me!"

"Life support is off inside the pod—he's run out of air," said Kit. "I can't tell about the suit."

"Are the pod's engines still functional?"

"Primary fuel is expended. Maneuvering jets look like they're still online."

"Can you activate the remote control program?" Elín asked.

"I can, but the jets won't be strong enough to stabilize the orbit, at least not for long."

"Just make it long enough, Kit." She shifted course, her fingers light on the jet controls.

Timms came into the cockpit. "Engines are gone, Halls. Jets is all we've got."

"That's all we need. Get down to docking port two. Kit is guiding the exo-pod in by remote."

"We found him? Christ, that's good news. Docking port two." He ran out of the room.

"Brace yourselves—here comes the front end of the blast," said Kit, his voice tight. "We're still only in partial shadow—"

The ship lurched, and the gravity cut off for a moment, giving Elín's stomach a turn. The lights dimmed, power faded. Just stay on course. She nudged the jet controls. *Stay with us, Solomon.*

The coronal plasma roared around them. The ship twisted, rolled. There was nothing she could do but wait, wait, as the solar storm raged past.

Finally their motion stabilized, and power came back up. Elín released a breath she didn't realize she'd been holding. The gray moon filled the cockpit window from the right, the uneven landscape of a barren world so close and in full detail. She couldn't see the sun.

The planet hung at the left edge of her field of vision, blue and bright and hot. And the Ring—so small it seemed, infinitesimal, dwarfed by the growing planet and the vast distance.

"Kit," she said, her voice sounding thin to her ears. "Where's the pod?"

"Off course. And so are we. But I've still got a remote lock. I'm bringing it in."

Elín snapped her attention back to her console, and fired up the maneuvering jets again, following the indicator of the pod. Closer, closer...

"Contact," said Kit.

"Got him!" Timms' voice over the comm. "Exo-pod is docked, port airlock is sealed and engaged."

Elín put her hand on Kit's shoulder as she stood up. "Keep us in a steady orbit around the moon, Kit. I'll be in the docking bay."

Timms was dragging a limp form out of the exo-pod into the bay. The indicator lights on the chest of the EVA suit glowed yellow. Elín knelt down and unfastened his helmet. "Bards."

She bent over him, touching his neck, listening for a breath. "He's got a pulse, very weak. He was almost out of air. Help me get him to the infirmary."

Timms laid Bards down on his side on the infirmary bed so that Elín could disconnect the air tank. Then they rolled him over on his back, and Elín pulled down a breathing mask and switched on the oxygen.

"Low oxygen and high CO2 in his blood," said Timms, nodding at the monitor attached to the bed. "But otherwise he looks okay. It looks like the moon and the exo-pod's shielding protected him well enough from the CME. We got him in time."

Elín held the mask against Bards' face, waiting for a voluntary deep breath, a flutter of eyelids. His dark skin was cold to the touch; she laid her fingers on his temple, wanting to share her warmth.

"Halls," said Kit's voice over the comm. "We've got an incoming long-range message."

She looked at Timms. "Stay with him." She slipped the mask strap around Bards' head. "I'll be right there, Kit."

In the cockpit, the comm screen flashed with the logo of Central Command. Bards' message had made it through. She hit the button.

"This is the Command ship *Alliance*. We're responding to a distress signal from the Epsilon Omega system. What is your status?"

Elín closed her eyes and released a breath. She spoke clearly, feeling strength in her voice. "This is cargo ship 1247-B53, out of Dyson-Vanderklein Habitable Ring Array. I am First Lieutenant Elín Hallsdóttir. We've sustained heavy damage to both our ship and the hyper-driver transport. We're dead in space, *Alliance*."

"Acknowledged. How many crew? Do you have injuries?"

Five. "Four crew." *Chang.* "One with minor injuries. We are treating him onboard."

"Acknowledged, cargo ship 1247. We have a fix on your coordinates and will arrive in three hours twenty-three minutes. Stand by, First Lieutenant."

"Acknowledged, *Alliance*." Elín shut off the comm.

She looked at Kit. His thin face was bright with relief, eyes soft behind his shaggy bangs. She smiled at him. "Good work, Kit. Just keep us in orbit around the moon."

He grinned. "Yes, ma'am."

"I'll be in the infirmary."

Timms was hunched over Bards' bed when Elín stepped in. He straightened up and looked at her.

"His oxygen levels are almost back to normal, but he's still unconscious. Should we give him a stim?"

Elín shook her head. "Let him be a little longer. I'm sure he'll wake up on his own." She came up next to the bed. "That was Command. Bards' signal got through. A ship will be here in a little over three hours."

Timms shut his eyes and ran a hand through his hair, then rubbed at his beard. "Finally. We're actually going home."

Home. Elín looked at Timms, then down at Bards. Home was behind her now.

"Why don't you get back to the cockpit and make sure everything's set for docking," she said. "I'll keep an eye on Bards."

Timms smiled. "Sure thing."

He left the room, and Elín pulled the nurse's stool over to Bards' bedside. He was still trapped in the bulky EVA suit, but she didn't want to even try to get him out of it until he was awake. She held his hand, knowing he wouldn't be able to feel her touch through the suit.

She laid her fingers against his temple again. His skin was warm now. "Bards," she said quietly. "We did it. *You* did it. A ship is coming for us. It's almost time to go...home."

———

STANDARD DAY CYCLE 13, 05:10 GST

Bards still slept, peacefully now. The med monitor showed rhythmic blue lines—natural sleep, not oxygen-deprived unconsciousness. Elín had removed the breathing mask. Perhaps she should give him a stim, as Timms had suggested hours ago. The Command ship would be here soon. She touched his face.

He moved his head. His eyes blinked, squinted, then opened; his dark irises rolled around, taking in the room, then settled on her face.

"Halls?" he said, his voice a quiet rasp. "What happened?" He coughed.

She got up and pulled a water pouch out of one the cupboards. She slipped her hand under his head to help him take a sip.

He coughed again. "Thanks." His voice was stronger now. "What happened? I'm still in my suit."

"Another CME came," she said. "You'd maneuvered your pod behind the moon and were protected from the blast. But you ran out of air. It looks like you'd set your suit's oxygen to half, but even that was almost depleted by the time we got to you."

"That must be why my head is pounding. So have you heard anything from Command yet? I sent a distress call and got an acknowledgement. I tried to contact you, but I don't think it got through."

"We got one transmission from you. Too full of static to understand anything except that you were alive. We couldn't raise you on a reply." She smiled. "But we're okay. A ship is on the way."

A shudder went through the floor, and Elín heard a distant clank. Timms' voice came over the comm. "Halls, the *Alliance* is here. They're bringing us in to their driver transport."

"Thank you, Timms," said Elín into her wrist-gear.

Bards looked up at Elín and gave a little smile. "That was fast."

She touched his arm. "You've been asleep for three hours. I wanted to let you wake up naturally; I figured you could use the sleep."

He smiled. "Thanks. Guess I needed it." He struggled to sit up. "Halls, help me get this suit off."

She helped him to stand, and then unclamped the seals so he could climb out of the suit. Then he stripped off the thermal layer.

"Much better," he said. "At least I can move my arms."

Elín felt the ship shudder again, this time as the *Alliance's* driver transport shifted into hyperspace. She looked at Bards.

"Good job, Lieutenant," he said with a smile. "You saved us."

"No, Bards. It was your message that went through. It was your idea to take a pod out to the comm array. You saved us."

He wrapped his arms around her neck and shoulders and pulled her against his chest in an embrace. She slid her arms around him and buried her face in his shoulder. He tightened his arms, putting one hand on the back of her head and holding her closer. No redshift.

"It won't be long now, Elín," he said softly. "We'll be back at Central Command, and then I'm going to take you home."

She lifted her head from his shoulder, just enough to look at him. *Home.* It was time to move forward. She rested her head again on his warm shoulder. "Yes, Solomon," she whispered. "Let's go home."

ABOUT THE AUTHOR:

Grace E. Robinson is an author and daydreamer, loves writing and finding joy in the little things in life. She lives in Idaho, surrounded by mountain views and a lot of books. She loves fantasy & folktales, sci-fi & creativity, nature & whimsy.

Read Grace's blog at her website, StorytellerGirlGrace.com[1].

---

1. https://storytellergirlgrace.com/